Storybook
Collection

This edition published by Parragon Books Ltd in 2014

Parragon Books Ltd
Chartist House
15–17 Trim Street
Bath BA1 1HA, UK
www.parragon.com

ISBN 978-1-4723-5697-0

Printed in China

Disney
Sofia the First

Storybook
Collection

PaRRagon

Bath • New York • Cologne • Melbourne • Delhi
Hong Kong • Shenzhen • Singapore • Amsterdam

Contents

Once Upon a Princess

Once upon a time, in the kingdom of Enchancia, there lived a little girl named Sofia. She and her mother, Miranda, didn't have much but their shoe shop, but they were happy.

One morning, Sofia and her mother went to the castle to bring King Roland a new pair of shoes. He and Miranda took one look at each other and it was love at first sight.

The couple married and soon Sofia and her mum were off to the castle for a life they never could have imagined.

Miranda lovingly greeted the king's children, Princess Amber and Prince James. Then she gave them each a brooch she had embroidered with their family crest.

King Roland placed a tiara on Sofia's head. "Welcome to the family!"

At dinner that evening, Sofia counted six different forks by her plate! Silverware clattered to the floor as she picked up one fork, then another.

King Roland could see it was going to take a while for Sofia to get used to her new royal life. He had a surprise to help her feel welcome. "We will be throwing a royal ball in your honour at week's end. You and I shall dance the first waltz."

Sofia was excited – she'd never been to a ball before!
But she was still nervous about becoming a princess.
"I think it's going to take me a while to get the hang of
things around here," said Sofia.

Amber nodded. "Just follow my lead and you'll be okay."

Sofia was grateful. Her new sister was going to help her
learn everything she needed to know – or so she thought!

Later on, Sofia went to her mum's room. "I don't know anything about being a princess. And I don't know how to dance. I'm going to trip and everyone's going to laugh at me."

Miranda smiled down at Sofia and assured her daughter that she'd be fine if she just tried her best.

Just then, they heard a knock at the door. It was King Roland – with a beautiful gift for Sofia!

"It's a very special amulet. So you must promise to never take it off," King Roland said.

Meanwhile, Amber had crept up to the door and overheard everything. She began to grow jealous of her new sister.

"Now you best run off to bed. You have princess school in the morning," said King Roland.

Princess school! Sofia liked the sound of that. Maybe she could learn how to act like a real princess in time for the ball after all!

As Sofia skipped back to her room, she bumped into Cedric. The royal sorcerer's beady eyes went straight to the amulet around Sofia's neck.

It was the Amulet of Avalor – the powerful charm Cedric had been trying to get for years! With its magic, he could overthrow King Roland and rule Enchancia. Cedric immediately began to plot how he'd trick Sofia into giving it to him.

The next morning, Sofia joined Amber and James for the coach ride to Royal Prep Academy. The headmistresses – Flora, Fauna and Merryweather – greeted her at the gates. At school, Sofia didn't need to worry about making friends. The other children liked her a lot – which made Amber even more jealous. She was used to being the popular one! Amber turned to James. "I think it's time Sofia took a ride on the magic swing."

So James led Sofia to the swing. "Try it! You don't have to kick. It swings itself."
Sofia climbed onto the swing. She was enjoying the ride until the swing
sped up and sent her flying into the fountain! Sofia put on a brave smile while
the other kids laughed, but James could tell she was upset. He felt terrible
about tricking his new sister.

When Sofia arrived home from her awful day at school, Cedric was waiting. "How would you like a private tour of my workshop? Not even the king himself has seen it!"

In one of Cedric's books, Sofia saw a picture of the Amulet of Avalor. "That looks just like my amulet!"

"No, it can't be! If you had the Amulet of Avalor, you'd know, for it contains powerful magic. Can I take a look at it?" Cedric said, sneakily.

Sofia shook her head. "I promised never to take it off."

As soon as Cedric realised his plan wasn't working, he rushed her out of his workshop. This was going to be tougher than he thought.

The next morning Sofia awoke to find a rabbit called Clover and
his bird friends, Robin and Mia, on her bed. They had come to help
her get ready and – thanks to the powers of her amulet – Sofia could
understand every word they were saying!

After breakfast with her new animal friends, Sofia left for Royal Prep.
She hoped her second day would be better!

Sofia tried hard in all her classes, but she went home feeling
discouraged again. "I thought being a princess would be easy. But it's
really hard," she told her mum.

Miranda had a surprise. She led Sofia to the patio, where her two
best friends, Jade and Ruby, were waiting at a fancy table set for tea.
Sofia was so glad to see them!

James joined the party, too. He still felt bad about tricking Sofia and
wanted to make it up to her.

Soon Sofia was curtsying and pouring tea like a proper princess, but she told James she still didn't know how to dance.

"No problem. We have dance class with Professor Popov tomorrow. You'll be dancing circles around all of us."

Amber had been watching everyone have fun without her. Now she was even more jealous of her stepsister. She had to make sure Sofia didn't dance better than she did.

The next day, before dance class, Amber gave Sofia a sparkling pair of dance slippers to wear.

Sofia put on the slippers, which immediately took control of her feet. She spun helplessly across the floor until the music ended and she collapsed into a pile of pillows.

Amber shrugged. "I must have grabbed a pair of Cedric's trick shoes by mistake. Sorry about that."

Sofia decided she couldn't chance another disaster at the ball – princesses just didn't go crashing into things – so when they got home, she went to Cedric for help.

"I have just the spell for you." He gave Sofia magic words to say when the waltz began. Little did she know that the spell would put everyone to sleep and help Cedric steal the amulet!

Soon it was time to get ready for the ball. Amber was admiring herself in the mirror when James came in.

"You gave Sofia the trick shoes on purpose. You're trying to ruin her ball because everyone likes her more than you. And after what you did today, so do I!"

"James! Come back!" Amber went after him – and accidentally tore her gown! How could she go to the ball now?

Sofia stood in front of her own mirror and stared at herself in her fancy gown and glittering tiara. She felt like a real princess!

For the first time that week, Sofia was actually looking forward to the ball!

A little while later, everyone watched as King Roland proudly escorted a beaming Sofia into the ballroom.

The orchestra began to play. It was time for the first waltz!

Sofia confidently spoke the magic words Cedric had given her:

"*Somnibus populi cella.*" Everyone instantly fell asleep – including Cedric!

"I must have said it wrong!" Sofia cried and ran out of the ballroom.

It seemed as if ever since she had become a princess, she couldn't do anything right.

Sofia sank to the floor and cried. A single tear fell on to her amulet and made it glow. Suddenly, a blue light appeared – and transformed into Cinderella!

"Your amulet brought me here. It links all the princesses that ever were. When one of us is in trouble, another will come to help," Cinderella explained. "Why are you so sad, Sofia?"

Sofia told Cinderella about trying to use a magic spell to help her become a better princess.

Cinderella smiled as she explained that she wasn't always a princess, either. But she discovered that the people who truly cared about you didn't care which fork you used or how well you danced.

Cinderella couldn't undo the spell, but she suggested that Sofia ask
her new sister for help. "Perhaps all she needs is a second chance."
Then Cinderella disappeared!
Sofia went to Amber's room. "I've done something terrible," Sofia explained.

She told her stepsister about the spell and then led her to the ballroom.
When Amber saw her father she gasped in shock!

Sofia felt terrible. "It's all my fault."

Amber shook her head. "No, Sofia. You wouldn't have needed the spell if
I hadn't given you those trick shoes."

The girls realized that what they really needed was each other.

They went to Cedric's workshop together to find a spell to wake everyone up but they had to get past Cedric's pet raven, Wormwood, first. Clover, Mia and Robin helped and soon the raven was locked in his cage. "Let's find that counterspell!"

Wormwood didn't realize that, with her amulet, Sofia could understand every word he said. So Clover tricked him into revealing where the counterspell book was hidden.

Now Cedric's spell could be broken!

Sofia and Amber were rushing to the ballroom when Amber remembered her torn dress. "I can't go in there looking like this," she sighed.

But Sofia wasn't about to leave her sister behind. She quickly mended the gown. "There you go. Good as new!"

Now it was Amber's turn to help. She led her sister in a waltz until Sofia was ready for the ball.

Sofia smiled as she took her place beside the king and recited the spell: "*Populi cella excitate!*" To her relief, everyone woke up.

Cedric was furious that his plan had been ruined!
"Merlin's mushrooms!" he said, as he flicked his wand
and disappeared in a puff of smoke.

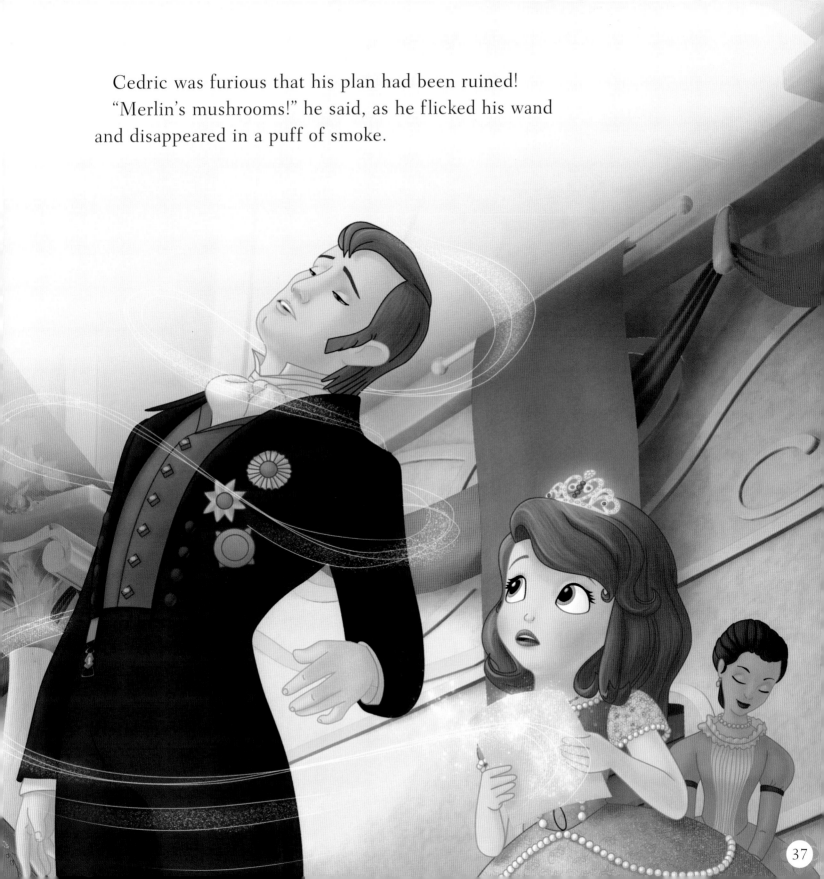

Meanwhile, Sofia and the king began to waltz.

Sofia looked up at her new dad. "I've been wondering. Why do they call you Roland the Second?"

The king explained to Sofia that his father had also been named Roland.

"So I guess that makes me Sofia the First!" she exclaimed.

And it was plain to see that this princess was going to live happily ever after!

The Royal
Slumber Party

Sofia and Amber are having a royal sleepover tonight!
"This is where we'll be sleeping," Amber says.
"The observatory? We get to sleep under the stars!" Sofia cries, happily.

"It's a royal slumber party," Amber explains. "Everything has
to be amazing."

Sofia's two best friends, Ruby and Jade, are coming.

Amber is shocked. "You invited girls from the village? You're a
princess now. You should only invite princesses to royal parties!"

"But Ruby and Jade are fun!" Sofia assures Amber. "You'll see."

The royal herald's trumpet sounds.

"They're here!" Sofia cries.

Amber's friends, Princess Hildegard and Princess Clio, step out of their coaches. Behind them are Jade and Ruby in a wooden cart.

"I can't believe we're here!" Jade exclaims, hugging Sofia.

"We're so excited!" Ruby adds.

It's time for the party to start! The princesses change into fancy nightgowns. Ruby and Jade giggle as they roll their hair in pinecone curlers – just like at home.

"We're at a royal sleepover!" they chant, pulling Sofia up to join their silly dance.

The other princesses stare at Ruby and Jade.
"What are they wearing?" Hildegard asks.
"What are they doing?" Clio wonders aloud.
Amber frowns. "Are those pinecones?"
Ruby hears her and dances over. "Want one? We brought extras."

Amber marches over to Sofia. "Sofia! Pinecones are not part of
a perfect princess sleepover."

Sofia's worried. She wants her new sister and her old friends to
like each other.

"They can fit in," she says. "They just need a little help."

Sofia has a great idea. "How would you two like a royal makeover?" she asks her friends.

Ruby and Jade squeal with excitement!

Baileywick and Sofia's woodland friends help out. They fix the girls' hair and dress them in pretty gowns and tiaras.

Sofia makes her friends cover their eyes. Then she leads them to a mirror. "Open your eyes," she says.

Jade and Ruby gasp when they see themselves. "I'm a princess!" Ruby exclaims.

"Me, too!" calls Jade.

Next it's time for party activities. First comes fan decorating.
Ruby and Jade have fun. But their fans don't look very princessy.
Then the girls play a game of Pin the Tail on the Unicorn.
"Ooh! Ooh!" Jade says. "Can I go first?"
But Jade ends up nowhere near the unicorn!

After that, the girls watch the royal sorcerer, Cedric, put on a magic puppet show in the banquet hall. During the show, James, Sofia's brother, walks in with a message for the girls.

"Prince James!" Jade and Ruby squeal as they rush towards him. They're thrilled to see the friendly prince!

But Jade and Ruby are so excited they accidentally knock over the chocolate-milk fountain. Oops! Chocolate milk splashes on to Amber's nightgown. She is furious!

"We're so, so, so sorry!" Ruby says to Amber.

"So sorry," Jade adds.

Amber walks off in a huff while Sofia shakes her head sadly.

Baileywick hurries Jade and Ruby away to get cleaned up.
Then James tells the girls it's time for dancing in the throne room.
"Let's go," Amber says. "Maybe we can enjoy five minutes of our party without Sofia's friends making a mess."

Now Sofia's even more worried! She goes off to find her friends.
"I want you both to fit in with the princesses," Sofia explains.

"We look just like them now, don't we?" Jade says.

"Yes," Sofia says. "But princesses don't talk so much, or laugh so loud, or make so much mess."

Jade frowns. "We were just having fun."

"We're sorry," Ruby adds quickly. "We'll try to act more like Amber and the other princesses."

Sofia is relieved. "Thank you!" Now she's sure everyone will get along!

Sofia and her friends join the others in the throne room. But Ruby and Jade don't know how to waltz. All they can do is stand and watch the princesses dance. After a while, they tell Sofia that they want to go home.

"But you're finally fitting in!" Sofia cries. "And you're not embarrassing me!"

"I'm sorry if we talk too much and laugh too loudly for your fancy new friends," says Jade. "Maybe we shouldn't be friends any more!"

Ruby takes Jade's arm and together they rush out of the room.
"Don't worry about them," Hildegard tells Sofia. "You're with us now."

Sofia goes after her friends but finds her mother instead. "I was trying to help Jade and Ruby fit in," she explains. "But I just made them feel bad."

"A true princess treats people with kindness, Sofia," Queen Miranda says gently. "If someone is your friend, you should like them for who they are."

Sofia knows her mother is right. She runs outside and finds her friends as they are about to leave.

"I'm sorry about the way I acted," she says. "Please let me make it up to you. We can have our own sleepover party – just the three of us!"

Jade and Ruby think for a moment and agree to stay.

Soon Sofia and her friends are in her room, having a great time. They laugh loudly. They talk a lot. They roll pinecones in their hair and perch tiaras on top.

Meanwhile, Amber and her friends go back to the observatory.

"Finally, it's just us princesses," Amber says.

"This is a perfect party," Hildegard agrees with a yawn.

There's a long silence. The princesses are really bored.

Clio speaks up, "You know, Sofia's friends were kind of fun."

A moment later, Amber and her friends knock on Sofia's door.
"Um, do you have room for a few more princesses?" asks Amber.
Sofia looks at Jade and Ruby. "What do you think?"
"The more, the merrier," Ruby says with a smile.
Sofia and Amber end up having the perfect sleepover with their friends – old and new!

The Amulet
and the Anthem

It's a special day in Enchancia. Sofia is at the stadium with Jade and Ruby. "Every kid in the kingdom will be here!" Sofia exclaims.

"Being chosen to sing the Enchancian anthem at the Harvest Festival is a big deal," Ruby says.

Ruby and Jade both hope their names will be chosen. They practise singing the anthem together while they wait.

"You two sound amazing!" Sofia cries.

Luciano, the host of the event, takes the stage. "It's the moment you've been waiting for," he says. "This year's singer will be…." Luciano picks a name out of a drum. "Princess Sofia!"

"Congratulations!" Jade says. Ruby gives Sofia a big hug. Then Luciano calls her up on to the stage.

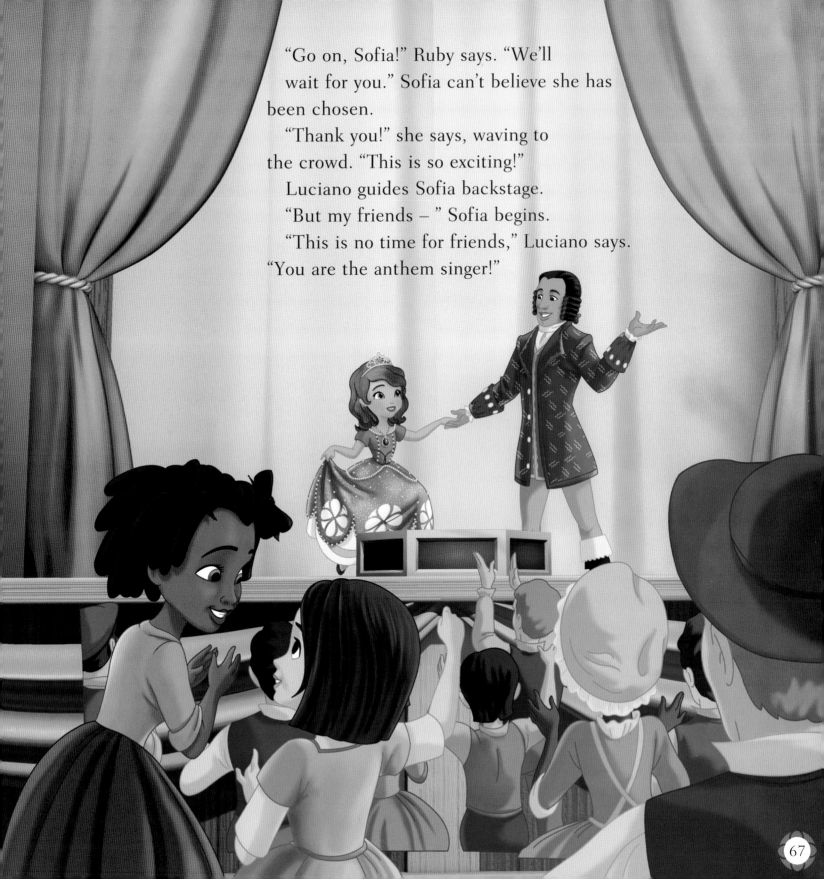

"Go on, Sofia!" Ruby says. "We'll
wait for you." Sofia can't believe she has
been chosen.

"Thank you!" she says, waving to
the crowd. "This is so exciting!"

Luciano guides Sofia backstage.

"But my friends – " Sofia begins.

"This is no time for friends," Luciano says.
"You are the anthem singer!"

While Sofia prepares for the big day, Ruby and Jade wait patiently for her outside.

"I'm so sorry!" Sofia cries, running up to her friends later. "I couldn't get away until now."

"That's okay," Ruby says. "How was it?"

"Unbelievable!" Sofia exclaims. "They gave me this hat and they're going to send hundreds of gowns to the castle and...."

Sofia goes on and on, bragging about her day. She's so excited she doesn't notice that her friends look hurt.

She also doesn't notice when her amulet starts to glow....

Sofia returns to the stage to rehearse her song. She opens her mouth to sing – but after a few words she lets out a loud, froggy "*Croak!*"

Sofia isn't sure what happened. "I'm a bit tired," she tells Luciano. "But don't worry, I know 'O Enchancia' by heart."

"All right," Luciano says. "Get some rest, and we'll see you at the festival tomorrow."

"Thank you – *croak!*" Sofia covers her mouth and rushes off stage.
Back at the castle, Sofia finds Clover and tells him what happened.
"What do you think is – *croak!* – wrong with me?" she cries.
Clover looks worried. "You've been cursed!" he says.

Sofia realizes she needs Cedric's help. When she tells him what has happened, the sorcerer says her amulet must have caused it.

"I thought my amulet only gave me magical powers," Sofia says.

"How soon you forget!" Cedric clears his throat and recites:

"'With each deed performed, for better or worse, a power is granted, a blessing – or curse.'"

Sofia is stunned. "The amulet cursed me – *croak!*"
she tells Clover. "Because I did something that wasn't nice."

"We've got to figure out what you did," Clover says.
"Maybe that will undo the curse."

But by the next morning, they still haven't figured it out. "I've got an idea," Clover says at last. "We've got to hop back and go over everything you did yesterday."

Sofia leads Clover all through the castle and then to the stadium. She remembers Luciano calling her on to the stage …

and getting her portrait painted …

and being interviewed …

and showered with gifts.

"Then I remembered Jade and Ruby were waiting for me," Sofia says. "I ran and told them about everything. I was so excited – *croak!* That's when it started."

Nearby, Sofia hears Amber bragging to her friends about the time she was chosen to sing the anthem.

"She sounds like … me!" Sofia realizes. "I was bragging to Ruby and Jade. I bet I made them feel bad, Clover. That must be why I'm cursed!"

Sofia quickly changes into her Harvest Festival gown and then runs to find her friends. "I shouldn't have bragged about being the anthem singer," she says. "I'm really sorry if I hurt your feelings."

To Sofia's relief, Ruby and Jade forgive her.

But after Sofia leaves her friends, she lets out another loud "*Croak!*"

Oh, no! It's almost time for her performance – and she's still cursed! Sofia isn't sure what to do.

Suddenly, her amulet glows again and Princess Belle appears!

Sofia tells Belle what has happened. "Can you help me?" she asks.

Belle smiles. "The only person who can undo the curse is you, Sofia," she says. "Someone I love did something unkind and was cursed, too. He looked into his heart and gave up something he wanted to show that he was truly sorry."

Sofia thinks about Belle's words.

"Look into my heart ... give up something," she murmurs.

"I think I know what to do, Belle!"

But Princess Belle is already gone.

Suddenly, Sofia hears Luciano introducing her.

"Hi, everyone," she says, running on to the stage. "I wish I could sing today. But – *croak!* – I have a frog in my throat."

The crowd gasps.

"It's okay," Sofia says. "I wasn't – *croak!* – nice to my friends yesterday and I want to make it up to them. Ruby and Jade, will you come up and sing the Enchancian anthem?"

As soon as Jade and Ruby start to sing Sofia's amulet glows once more. "I did it!" Sofia whispers to Clover. "The curse is gone."

Then Ruby and Jade pull Sofia over to join them. And not a croak can be heard as the three friends sing 'O Enchancia' together.

The Royal Games

One beautiful day in Enchancia, three grand coaches coast to a landing at the royal picnic grounds. The herald announces the arrival of three royal families from three different kingdoms: Wei-Ling, Khaldoun and Enchancia.

"The Tri-Kingdom Picnic is no ordinary picnic," Amber tells Sofia as they climb out of their family's coach.

Sofia looks around at all the people, the fancy tent and the buffet table piled high with delicious food. "I'm starting to see that!" she says.

"Sofia!" James exclaims, running over. "You've got to see this."
He leads her to a huge trophy – the Golden Chalice.

"All the kids at the picnic play games and the kingdom
that wins the most games gets to keep the chalice until the
next picnic," James says. "I've always wanted to win it!"

James explains that Amber doesn't like playing the games.
He's hoping that Sofia can take her place this year.

"Teammates?" James asks.

Sofia smiles. "Teammates!"

Sofia and James change their clothes. Then they meet the kids from the other families: Princess Maya and Prince Khalid of Khaldoun, and Princess Jun and Prince Jin of Wei-Ling.

Baileywick announces the start of the first game – the Flying Horseshoe Toss.

At first Sofia doesn't understand why it's called Flying Horseshoe Toss. Then she sees the wings on the horseshoes! That makes the game extra tricky, since the horseshoes like to fly off course!

Jin goes first and his horseshoe lands nowhere near the stake.

"Good try, Jin!" Maya says.

Jun's horseshoe lands on the buffet table. "Oops!" she giggles. "Someone tell my horseshoe it's not time for lunch."

Then it's James's turn. His horseshoe lands near the stake. "Best throw so far!" Jin says.

Princess Maya goes next. Her horseshoe lands even closer to the stake than James's!
"Nice one," Khalid says.
"Sofia, it's up to you," James says. "If you get closer than Maya, we win."

CLANG! Sofia's horseshoe hits the stake!
"Way to throw!" Maya cheers.
Sofia jumps up and down. "I did it!" she cries.
"Enchancia wins!" Baileywick announces.

"Nicely done, Sofia," Jin says.

James points at the others. "We won! I've never won before! We're the best!" he shouts. "Enchancia's going to win this year!"

"All right, we heard you," Jin says.

James ignores him. "Come on, Sofia. Let's go win the next game!" he cries, rushing off.

Sofia is surprised by the way James is acting. "He's just really excited," she tells the others with a sheepish smile.

Maya frowns. "I guess so."

"Time for the Golden Egg on a Silver Spoon race," Baileywick calls.

Sofia balances her golden egg carefully. When Baileywick says, "Go,"
she races on to the course.

SPLAT! SPLAT! Jun and Khalid drop their eggs within moments.
Maya stumbles and almost loses hers but catches it just in time.

"Nice save," Sofia tells her.

"Sofia!" James says. "This is a race. There's no time to talk!"
But this distracts Sofia and – SPLAT! – she drops her egg.

James and Maya keep going. James almost wins, but at the last
second Maya passes him and crosses the finish line in first place.

Everyone congratulates Maya – everyone except James, that is. He throws his egg to the ground. SPLAT!

"I would have won except the sun was in my eyes!" he complains.

"What a sore loser," Maya whispers to Jun.

Sofia hears her. "Sorry again," she says. "I'll talk to James."

Sofia finds him getting ready for the next game. "Could you be a little nicer to the other kids?" she suggests.

"I'm not doing anything wrong," James insists. "I'm just trying to win."

"But, James…." Sofia begins.

It's no use. James is already rushing off.

The next game is Tri-Kingdom Triplenet.

James plays hard, doing everything he can to keep the ball from touching the ground on Enchancia's side of the triangle. In the end, James and Sofia are the winners.

"We won and you lost!" he jeers at the other teams afterwards.

Sofia tries to stop James from taunting them. But he won't listen.

"We don't want to play any more," Maya says at last.

"We don't, either," Jin agrees. "If you want the chalice so badly, you can have it. We quit."

"Sorry, Sofia," Jun adds.

James shrugs. "I don't get it. Why is everyone quitting?" he asks Sofia.

"Because they're not having any fun," Sofia says. "You've been a bad sport all day. I don't want to be your teammate any more."

"Sofia!" James exclaims, sounding upset. "Come back!"

As Sofia hurries away, she notices the adults playing a game nearby. They're all laughing and having fun. None of them seem to care who is winning.

That gives Sofia an idea....

"There's something you need to see," Sofia tells James. She drags
him over to watch the adults play Bewitching Bowling. James sees
his dad mess up his turn – and laugh!

"Oh, well," King Roland says. "Better luck next time – I hope!"

"See?" Sofia says to James. "Games are supposed to be fun –
whether you win or lose."

"I guess I haven't been much fun to play with," says James.

James finds the other kids and apologises for being a sore loser – and a sore winner. "I forgot that the Tri-Kingdom Picnic is all about getting together and having a good time. I'm really sorry."

The kids decide to forgive James and the games continue.

At the end of the day, Khaldoun wins the Golden Chalice.
Sofia is happy to see that nobody cheers louder than James.
"Maybe we'll win next year," she tells him. "Teammates?"
He grins and shakes her hand. "Teammates!"

The Halloween Ball

Sofia is so excited. King Roland and Queen Miranda – Dad and Mum – are hosting a Halloween ball!

Everybody will create a fancy costume to wear and, even better, there will be prizes! Sofia can't wait to get started!

The girls draw some of their ideas for their costumes.
Amber really wants to win the Best Costume prize.
"I'm going to be a peacock," she tells Sofia.
"I'm sure you'll be the prettiest peacock ever!" says Sofia.

Amber tries to make her costume but the feathers end up everywhere except on her skirt. And with her hat on, she looks more like a cockerel than a peacock.

Amber goes to find Sofia for help. "Can you make my costume look like this?" she says, holding out her sketch.

"I'll do my best!" Sofia says with a smile. She carefully stitches some pretty feathers to Amber's skirt and a pink cape. Then she creates a matching cap of feathers. Sofia leads Amber to the mirror.

"Ta-da!" she cries.

Amber gives Sofia a hug when she sees herself. "Thank you!" she says. "I'm definitely going to win the prize!"

Now Sofia has to make her own fairy costume.

First she stitches together a fancy skirt. Next she glues on sparkly
wings. To finish it off, she makes a tiny crown of flowers. It's perfect!
Sofia can't wait to wear her costume to the ball!

The day of the Halloween ball finally arrives. But when Amber sees Sofia
in her costume, she gets upset. Her sister's costume is even better than hers!
"I'll just have to make my costume fancier," Amber says under her breath.
First she'll add more feathers … and she knows just where to find them.

On his way to the party, James spots Amber outside collecting peacock feathers. "What in the world are you doing?" he calls down to her. "It's time for the ball!"

With an armful of feathers, Amber rushes back to the castle. But on the way, she slips and falls into a muddy puddle!

Meanwhile, all the guests have arrived and are waiting in the ballroom.

"Where is Amber?" Sofia asks her brother.

Sofia follows a trail of muddy footprints to Amber's room.
"What happened?" asks Sofia.

"I was jealous of your costume," Amber explains.
"And I wanted to make mine better. I'm sorry."

"I understand," Sofia says softly.

"Now look at me," says Amber. "I can't go to the ball!"

"Yes, you can," says Sofia. "We'll think of something. I don't want to go without you."

After a minute, Sofia cries, "I've got it! I can share my costume with you!"

"I don't understand," Amber replies, shaking her head.

"You will," says Sofia.

Sofia has the perfect plan. She begins to take her costume apart and in no time she has a matching costume for Amber!

"See?" says Sofia.

"Now we're both fairies!" cries Amber.
"Twin fairies!" Sofia replies.
"Twin sister fairies!" adds Amber with a smile.

The girls hurry to the ballroom and arrive just in time for the costume parade!
The judges, Flora, Fauna and Merryweather, watch closely as each child
walks by.

Maya's rainbow costume wins the prize for Prettiest Costume.

Jin's jester costume wins the prize for Silliest Costume.

And the Best Costume prize goes to Khalid's dragon.

"Actually, there is one last prize," says Flora, "for the Most Thoughtful Costume."
Merryweather smiles as she presents the trophy to Sofia and Amber.
Now the sisters share a costume and a prize!
"But my real prize," says Amber, "is having a sister I can count on!"

Sofia's Magic Lesson

Sofia is so excited! It's her first sorcery class at Royal Prep.
"I can't wait to learn magic," she says, taking her seat next to James in the classroom.

Fauna, their sorcery teacher, explains that the first lesson is to learn a spell that will change a rock into a ruby.

Sofia gets ready to try the spell. She waves her wand, says the magic words and turns her rock into … an apple!

Sofia looks around and sees that all the other kids have rubies on their desks. "Don't worry, class," says Fauna. "You can practise at home later. We have three new spells to learn today."

Three new spells – plus a test at the end of the week! How will Sofia ever learn them all?

After school, Sofia practises her spells with Clover. This time she turns a rock into a tomato!

"It was supposed to turn into a ruby," she says, disappointed.

Clover grabs the tomato. "This is much better," he says, taking a big bite. "If you want to learn magic, ask a sorcerer!"

That's it! Cedric is just the person to help Sofia.

When Cedric sees Sofia at his door, he can't help staring at her magical amulet. "It's so nice to see your amulet – I mean, it's so nice to see you," he says, inviting her inside. As Sofia looks around at the mess in Cedric's workshop, she gets an idea. "Could I help clean up your workshop in return for magic lessons?" she asks.

Having Sofia in his workshop every day will give Cedric a chance to take the amulet! So he agrees to make Sofia his apprentice.

"I'm going to brew up a potion that will make me invisible," Cedric tells Wormwood after Sofia leaves. "Then I'll steal Sofia's amulet and use it to rule the kingdom!"

Wormwood squawks with delight.

"I will be King Cedric the First!" Cedric announces happily.

When Sofia returns the next day, she's ready for her first magic lesson. While Sofia cleans, Cedric works on his invisibility potion – it doesn't go very well, though.

Next Cedric teaches Sofia a phrase that his father, Goodwyn the Great, taught him: "Slow and steady does the trick." Sofia holds her wand straight and she slowly recites the magic words. It works! In her hand is a ruby!

"I did it!" Sofia exclaims. "You are a really good teacher, Mr Cedric."

Cedric blushes. He's not used to getting compliments.

Just then, Baileywick comes in with a message for Cedric. King Roland wants to see him right away.

Roland tells Cedric that King Magnus is coming for a visit. "He's always bragging about his kingdom," King Roland says. He points to the stone gargoyles. "Maybe you could change the gloomy gargoyles into golden horses. That would impress him!"

So Cedric raises his wand and turns a gargoyle into a winged horse … but it flies away! King Roland shakes his head. "Not every royal sorcerer can be as gifted as your father," he says.

Poor Cedric!

Back in Cedric's workshop, Sofia finishes cleaning.
"I'm sorry your spell didn't work," says Sofia.
Cedric shrugs. Then he tells Sofia about his father who was
the greatest royal sorcerer who ever waved a wand. "He even saved
King Roland's father nine times! But I haven't saved anyone's life."

Just then, one of the potion bottles falls over. It spills onto Sofia and transforms her into a lizard!

In an instant, Cedric leaps into action. "*Lizardo chango!*"

And – poof! – Sofia changes back.
"Thank you!" Sofia exclaims.
"Oh, that's an easy spell," Cedric says.

Sofia looks up at Cedric. "You're so good at magic. So why couldn't you turn the gargoyles into golden horses?"

Cedric admits that when he's around the king, he gets nervous.

"I'm going to find a way to show my dad that you're a great sorcerer," Sofia tells Cedric.

"Why would you do that?" Cedric asks.

Sofia grins. "Because you're my friend."

At dinner that night, King Magnus goes on and on about his kingdom and his sorcerer.

"We have a great sorcerer, too," Sofia says. "We should have him put on a show!"

Her family looks worried. After all, Cedric isn't really great at magic. But when King Magnus finds out that Cedric is the son of Goodwyn the Great, he insists.

Back in Cedric's workshop, Sofia encourages her friend.
"We can help each other get ready," she says. "Remember?
Slow and steady does the trick."

While Cedric is busy preparing tricks for his royal magic show, Sofia practises her spells for the sorcery test.

But her spells still aren't perfect.

A little bit later, as Sofia cleans Cedric's workshop, she wipes a smudge off his spell book and discovers why Cedric's invisibility potion isn't working. He didn't see two ingredients on the list!

When Sofia tells him the news, Cedric can't believe it!
Now he can finally make the potion! He says goodnight to Sofia,
drops the final two ingredients into the cauldron and smiles.
"I did it, Wormy!" he shouts.

And then Cedric sees what Sofia left for him.
"She made this for me?" Cedric asks. Nobody has
ever done anything like that for him before.

The next day Sofia is ready for her magic test!

Fauna passes out a rock, a lime and an old shoe. "You must perform the three transformation spells we learned this week," she says.

Sofia takes a deep breath and remembers Cedric's advice.
"Slow and steady," she tells herself.

It works! Sofia passes the sorcery test!

She runs home to show her mum and dad her gold star.

Meanwhile, Cedric is ready for the magic show. "When it's time for my last trick, I'll pour the invisibility potion on myself, swipe Sofia's amulet and take over the kingdom!" he tells Wormwood.

The magic show begins and Cedric announces his first trick will be to make Clover fly. But instead he makes poor Clover bounce around the room! King Roland shakes his head in disappointment.

Sofia feels bad for Cedric. 'If only he was doing a trick he knew well,' she thinks. Then she has an idea!

She takes the lizard potion from Cedric's magic bag and spills it on herself.

"Sofia's a lizard!" James shouts.

In a flash Cedric cries, "*Lizardo chango!*" and – poof! – Sofia is back, unharmed.

Cedric's next trick is the invisibility potion! "It's a trick I've been planning for many, many years," he says, raising his wand.

But then he sees Sofia's smiling face. He lowers his arm … and pours the potion on Clover instead!

Everyone, including King Magnus, is impressed. "Cedric is a great sorcerer!" he declares.

Back in Cedric's workshop, Sofia gives her friend a gold star.
"It was fun being your apprentice," she says. "Good night, Mr Cedric."
Cedric watches her leave and then turns to Wormwood. "Oh, Wormy,"
he says. "We can always take over the kingdom tomorrow."